DRAGON GIRLS

Naomi the Rainbow Glitter Dragon

by Maddy Mara

SCHOLASTIC

Published in the UK by Scholastic, 2022
Euston House, 24 Eversholt Street, London, NW1 1DB
Scholastic Ireland, 89E Lagan Road, Dublin Industrial Estate,
Glasnevin, Dublin, D11 HP5F

First published in the US by Scholastic Inc, 2021

Text © Maddy Mara, 2022
Illustrations by Thais Damião © Scholastic Inc., 2021

The right of Maddy Mara and Thais Damião to be identified
as the author and illustrator of this wzrk has been asserted by
them under the Copyright, Designs and Patents Act 1988.

ISBN 978 0702 31101 7

A CIP catalogue record for this book is available from the British Library.

Printed by CPI Group (UK) Ltd, Croydon, CR0 4YY
Paper made from wood grown in sustainable forests and other
controlled sources.

1 3 5 7 9 10 8 6 4 2

www.scholastic.co.uk

Book design by Stephanie Yang

Naomi grinned as she looked around the adventure park. This was her happy place, that was for sure! The park was bustling with people. Kids on skateboards performed tricks on the half-pipe. Others flew by on the zip line. The climbing wall was really busy too.

"You might have to wait in line for all the

good things today," said Naomi's dad. "I hope you don't get bored."

"I won't!" Naomi promised. "I want to practise my gymnastics routine anyway."

"Well, we'll be over at the picnic area," said her mum, unstrapping Naomi's baby brother, Dakari, from his stroller. "Come find us when you get hungry."

"OK!" Naomi called happily, running off.

Her dad had packed a delicious picnic, but Naomi was way too excited to eat. Lately, some amazing things had been happening to Naomi. *Magical* things. She had visited an incredible place called the Magic Forest. Everything in the Magic Forest seemed special and different – even Naomi herself!

When she entered the forest, she was no longer a normal girl. She became a Dragon Girl. This meant she could fly and had incredible dragon strength. Even better, her friends Azmina and Willa were Dragon Girls too. The three of them weren't just any Dragon Girls, either: they were GLITTER Dragon Girls!

Azmina was the Gold Glitter Dragon and Willa was silver. Naomi was the Rainbow Glitter Dragon – which made sense because Naomi loved colourful things. She liked wearing bright clothes, and her parents had finally let her paint one of her bedroom walls purple and another one green.

Naomi and her friends were helping protect the Magic Forest from the evil Shadow Sprites. The Shadow Sprites were troublemakers who wanted to change the forest into a grey and dull place. This would allow their cruel leader, the Shadow Queen, to return and take control. But the Dragon Girls were determined not to let that happen!

"I'll be down near the wall," Naomi called to her parents as she ran towards the old stone wall near the edge of the park. On the other side were the local woods. The trees rustled their leaves as Naomi got closer. It felt like they were waving at her.

Naomi sprang up lightly on to the sturdy wall. It was wider than the beam she used for gymnastics training, but it was still good practice. Expertly, Naomi flipped up on to her hands and began to walk along the wall upside down. The stones were smooth and warm to her touch.

Nearby, Naomi could hear the shouts of excited kids playing. But she could hear another sound too, and it was coming from the woods.

Magic Forest, Magic Forest, come explore...

Naomi lowered herself into a backbend, then stood up. Her heart beat very fast. The Magic Forest was calling her! She had been on a few adventures in the Magic Forest, and she got the same thrilling feeling every time.

She turned to look at the adventure park. It was alive with colour and sound and joy. Kids dashed from one piece of equipment to another. Over in the picnic area, Naomi could see her parents sitting on the grass with her little brother.

No one was paying any attention to her. Naomi grinned. Perfect! Quickly, she scanned the ground on the far side of the wall. It was autumn now, so most of the flowers were gone for the season. But Naomi spotted one, just as she knew she would.

At first, the flower seemed to be yellow. But when she moved her head, it suddenly looked pink. When she moved back the other way, the flower changed to a rich purple. Excitement bubbled inside her.

This was definitely *her* flower. In fact, it was more than that. It was her travel charm – her way into the Magic Forest. She crouched down and reached out her hand. The flower seemed to bend towards her. Gently, Naomi plucked the bloom. A honey-cinnamon scent filled the air. As Naomi brought the flower to her nose, it changed colour again. Now it was orange!

She breathed in the flower's delicate aroma. It smelled like the Magic Forest. Naomi shivered happily. Soon, very soon, she would be there again.

Naomi glanced over at the park. Her mother caught sight of her and waved. Naomi waved back, but inside she groaned. It was important that no one watch her right now. Then one of her mum's friends arrived. Naomi's mum turned towards her friend and started talking. *Phew!*

There wasn't a moment to lose. Naomi tucked

the flower (which was now bright red) behind her ear. She turned to face the woods as she heard the familiar words:

Magic Forest, Magic Forest, come explore...

"Magic Forest, Magic Forest, hear my roar!" finished Naomi.

She jumped up into the air. Mid-air somersaults were Naomi's all-time favourite move. And they were even more fun when she did them to get into the Magic Forest!

Everything seemed to happen in slow motion. It was like Naomi was floating in space, with no gravity to pull her down to the ground.

She felt the breeze on her face and her hair being pushed back. Naomi tucked her knees in even tighter as she spun through the air. She stretched out her legs and landed firmly on the ground. Perfect dismount!

The sounds of the park had faded. The busy playground had completely disappeared. Gone were the slides and the swings and the kids waiting for the zip line. The bloom from behind her ear had also disappeared, but Naomi knew her travel charm would reappear when it was time to return home.

She was surrounded by clusters of flowers, all swaying gently in the breeze. Trees grew thickly around her, tendrils of ivy winding up around their trunks. The noise of people had been replaced with a strange and magical birdsong.

But it wasn't just her surroundings that had changed. Naomi looked down. Her normal-girl feet had been replaced by powerful paws tipped with claws, each one a different hue.

Her smooth skin was gone, and she was now covered in scales and striped with colour. And best of all, a pair of mighty wings had appeared on her back. She was a Dragon Girl!

Naomi stretched out her wings and gave them a flap. Multicoloured specks of light whooshed into the air. The specks danced for a moment before gently falling to the ground like rainbow mist.

"Hi, Magic Forest," Naomi whispered to herself, spinning around. "It's so good to see you again!"

2

Naomi knew she had to hurry to the glade at the centre of the forest. This was the safe place where the Tree Queen lived. Willa and Azmina would also be on their way to the glade. They would be eager to discover what their next quest was too.

All the same, Naomi couldn't resist bending

down to smell the flowers growing all around her.

Naomi took a deep breath. The flowers smelled like a heady mix of sunshine, honey and magic. But then the scent began to fade. A moment later, the smell was completely gone. When Naomi took another breath, they smelled like ... cardboard. Even worse, the colour began to fade. Now the flowers were grey!

"What is going on?" Naomi cried in shock.

"It's the Shadow Queen and her tricky Shadow Sprites," said a nearby voice.

From behind a tree appeared the strangest, most delightful little bird Naomi had ever seen. She had gorgeous, bright tail feathers, and tiny wings that were all the colours of the rainbow. The bird's tail was long, almost like a pony's tail, and streamed out behind her. Her eyes twinkled in a friendly  way. Most curious of all, a tiny horn protruded from the bird's little forehead.

"My name's Unichick," chirped the creature, landing on a branch and giving a little bow. "Because of my unicorn horn, obviously. I'm here to help whenever you need me."

Naomi liked the little bird already. And she was very happy to hear Unichick was there to help! "The Shadow Sprites are stealing the colour from the flowers now?" she asked, frowning.

The sprites had already tried to take away the sunshine and the sparkle from the forest's waters.

Unichick flew closer. "Not just from the flowers. They're also taking it from the grasses and the trees – and all the berries and other fruits that grow in the forest."

Naomi looked around. Just moments before, the trees and plants around her had been bright and beautiful. Now she saw the colour slowly fading away. The grass beneath her paws, the leaves on the trees, even the ivy was gradually turning pale and grey.

Naomi's heart pumped faster. "We have to stop this!"

"Yes, and there isn't much time," said Unichick in her sing-song voice. "Have you noticed the sky?" Naomi glanced up and saw that the sky glowed red. "The sun is setting much earlier than usual," explained Unichick. "The Shadow Sprites are more powerful in the twilight, when the shadows are longer. It's going to be hard to outsmart them with the sun so low."

"There's no way we Glitter Dragons are letting those Shadow Sprites beat us," declared Naomi. "Come on, Unichick. Let's race to the glade."

The trees grew very close together in this part of the Magic Forest. It was hard for Naomi to see where she was flying. The strange red glow of the sky made it harder still. Luckily, Naomi's gymnastics gave her quick reflexes. She ducked underneath low-hanging branches and swooped around thorny bushes. Unichick stuck close to her side. The little creature's bright feathers seemed to glow, which helped Naomi see her way through the dense thicket.

It felt good to have the little bird with her because everywhere she looked, Naomi could see signs of the Shadow Sprites. Many of the tree trunks were concrete grey, and when she brushed against the leaves, they crumbled into ash-like dust. Sometimes she saw grey shapes slither from the undergrowth and curl up the trees. Wherever the shadowy shapes went, they left a faded streak behind them.

"The sprites are everywhere," Unichick cheeped. "They are determined to win this time."

"Don't worry," said Naomi. "Azmina, Willa and I will fix this. We're a great team." Just saying the words made Naomi feel stronger. The Glitter Dragon Girls could do anything – she was sure of it!

Up ahead, the branches of trees had formed a tunnel. The space was very narrow, but Naomi knew they needed to get through it. "Lucky

you're so tiny," she called to Unichick.

She pressed her wings close to her sides and whooshed at top speed towards the leafy pathway. Naomi felt a bit like a train heading through a mountain pass!

The tunnel was very dark. Twigs and branches

scraped at Naomi, but she kept zooming as fast as she could. She could see the end of the tunnel up ahead, so she knew the shimmering force field that protected the glade wasn't far.

Naomi grinned. "We're almost there, Unichick!"

But just as Naomi was coming out, everything went completely black. It was as if someone had turned out the lights. "Unichick? What's happening?" Naomi called, jolting to a stop in mid-air. Something cold and scratchy, like fine sandpaper, was pressing against her face.

"There's a sprite wrapped around your eyes!" Unichick cried out.

Naomi shook her head, but the sprite didn't

budge. She could feel all her confidence start to seep out of her. She was no longer sure that she and the other Dragon Girls would beat the Shadow Sprites. She wasn't even sure she'd make it to the glade!

What should I do? Naomi wondered. She knew that panicking would not help, but it was hard to stay calm.

She heard the hum of fast-beating wings in her ear. "You have to roar the sprite away!" Unichick chirped.

Of course! Naomi took in a huge gulp of air. Then she roared with all her might! She couldn't see her roar's rainbow glitter because it was so dark, but she could definitely hear the roar. The trees seemed to sway with the sound.

Taking another deep breath, Naomi roared again. This time, tiny holes began to appear in the shadows covering her eyes. She could see streaks of colour swirling in the air.

"That's it, Naomi!" Unichick sang excitedly. "It's working!"

Naomi took one final breath and roared as fiercely as she could. This time the shadowy blindfold dissolved completely.

"You did it!" trilled Unichick, doing happy loops in the air. "I knew you would."

"Thanks for your help," Naomi said, relieved. Now that the mask was gone from her eyes, she felt strong and confident again. But she had no doubt the Shadow Sprites would try their worst tricks during this quest. She and her friends would have to be very brave and very clever to beat them!

3

Naomi and Unichick flew to the edge of the glade. The force field that protected the glade buzzed with powerful magic. Naomi knew that Unichick wouldn't come in with her. Only those who had been summoned by the Tree Queen could pass through the force field. Naomi felt a little sad to say goodbye to the gorgeous bird. She already felt like a friend.

"I'll return when you need me," Unichick promised, as though she could hear Naomi's thoughts. "Good luck!"

With that, she fluttered away. Naomi took a deep breath and pressed through the force field. It always reminded her of passing a hand slowly through running water ... except the force field wasn't wet. The air inside the glade was warm and sweet-smelling. Naomi was relieved to see that within the glade, the plants were still colourful, and the flowers smelled just as they should.

"Hi, Naomi!" called a cheerful voice. "We just got here too."

Two Dragon Girls were hovering near the majestic tree in the centre. One silver and one gold – both dazzling. Naomi felt her heart leap. Willa was a very old friend from nursery and Azmina was a very new friend. It was so good to see them both!

The branches of the tree began to sway gently. As Naomi

watched, two branches softened into long,

elegant arms. The lower part of the trunk changed into a flowing gown. The upper part became a neck, and soon a kind, beautiful face appeared. The face was framed by long locks of wavy brown hair.

The Tree Queen stood before the Dragon Girls. She looked strong and healthy, but when she smiled, Naomi could see worry in her eyes.

"What's wrong, Tree Queen?" she asked, stepping forward. "You can tell us anything, you know."

"Ah, but that is exactly the problem," replied the queen, frowning. "I can't talk freely at all. Look!" The Tree Queen pointed one of her strong, flexible arms at the protective shield of the glade.

Naomi saw grey shapes moving across its surface. Were they clouds?

"Shadow Sprites!" Azmina gasped.

"Can they get in here?" Willa asked nervously.

"No," the Tree Queen assured them. "Here in the glade we are safe from harm. But I fear they can hear us. Normally, they cannot get so close to the force field. My magic is too powerful. But their Shadow Queen has created a long-lasting sunset, and the sprites can move almost anywhere. As you've all noticed, they are stealing the colour from the

trees and flowers of the forest. Some of the birds and butterflies are losing their colour too."

Naomi thought about Unichick's gorgeous multicoloured feathers. It was too terrible to think of her turning grey!

"But we can make a potion to stop them, right?" Naomi asked.

"There is a potion," the Tree Queen agreed, "but I can't tell you the ingredients. If the Shadow Sprites hear what you need to find, they will get to the ingredients first. And they will destroy what you require."

The Glitter Dragons looked at one another in dismay. How could they gather ingredients for a potion when they had no idea where to start? It didn't seem possible.

Then Naomi had an idea. Sometimes, on the way to school, her dad gave her logic puzzles to solve. Just yesterday, he'd asked, "Naomi, what goes up and up, but never comes down?"

That was an easy one, and Naomi had got it straight away. A person's age!

"Maybe you could tell us the ingredients as riddles?" she suggested to the Tree Queen.

"Yes!" Azmina nodded. "I bet we can work them out before the sprites do."

The Tree Queen rewarded Naomi with a broad smile. "That's an excellent suggestion. The sprites are devious, but they're not very clever. Certainly not as clever as you three! But they might ask the Shadow Queen for help. She might be shadowy, but she is also very bright."

"Naomi will work out the riddles faster than some shadowy queen," Willa said, wrapping a silver wing around Naomi's shoulder. "And we'll help."

Naomi grinned at her friend. She really hoped she could prove Willa right!

The Tree Queen fell silent for a moment, swaying gently as she considered her riddles. "To find the first ingredient," she said slowly, "you must aim high before you get to the root of the problem. Find the one who seems calm, but is actually petrified."

The shadows crawling across the force field began to slither around very quickly, making horrible sounds. It was clear they were angry.

Azmina nudged Naomi. "I hope you understand what that riddle means," she muttered. "Because I sure don't!"

"I'll figure it out," Naomi said.

"For the second ingredient, look for the ones who are feared but should be revered," continued the Tree Queen. "Do not be afraid of them. They don't have a leg to stand on and are completely harmless."

Naomi tried not to look worried. She had NO idea what any of this meant! These puzzles were totally different from the ones she did with her dad.

"And for your final clue: sweetness is held within my skin. But I am protected by many a pin," said the queen.

On the surface of the force field, the Shadow Sprites were whipping back and forth in a furious panic. Naomi felt like her insides were doing the same thing! But sometimes, when her dad gave her a really hard puzzle, she pushed it to the back of her mind for a while. It was like her brain kept working away on the problem, even when she wasn't aware that she was thinking about it. Maybe that would happen this time.

Willa put her paw on Naomi's. "Don't worry," she said. "We'll do this together, OK? It will be fine."

Naomi nodded gratefully. Thank goodness she was part of a team!

"You're in charge of this quest, Naomi. You'll need this." Willa handed Naomi the special bag she had worn during their last adventure. As it passed from her paw to Naomi's, the fabric changed from silver to rainbow. Naomi was nervous about being in charge, but she slipped on the bag.

"Take this too," said the Tree Queen, lowering one of her branches towards Naomi.

Dangling from the end was a tiny apple, no bigger than an acorn. But it didn't stay tiny for long. As Naomi watched, the apple grew and grew. Its skin swirled with colours like the surface of a bubble. When it had finished growing, the apple gently broke away from the stem and fell into Naomi's waiting paws. This was no apple for snacking on! It was a magic

apple. Naomi twisted
the leaf, and the apple
opened neatly into two
halves. Inside, it was
smooth and hollowed
out like a bowl. Naomi

put the lid back on and slipped the apple into
the rainbow-coloured bag.

Secretly, Naomi felt totally unsure about
what they needed to do to make their potion.
But there was no way she was going to show
her nerves – not while those Shadow Sprites
were listening in.

"Come on, Glitter Dragons! Let's go make a
potion," she roared, leaping up into the air to

scare off the sprites slithering along the surface of the force field. The sprites scattered in every direction as Willa and Azmina joined Naomi.

Naomi felt tingles of excitement. Together, they would beat those Shadow Sprites!

In Naomi's opinion, flying was the very best thing about being a Dragon Girl. It felt as natural to Naomi as running or walking. And it was *much* more fun. She loved practising mid-air gymnastics, doing backwards somersaults and forward rolls as she zoomed above the treetops. But today Naomi knew they had to stay focused on the mission ahead. Once the sun set, the Shadow Sprites would be even more powerful.

Naomi looked down at the forest below her. She couldn't see any Shadow Sprites right now, but she could definitely see their work. Many trees and flowers were completely grey, and the grass looked like it was dying. She frowned. They just *had* to stop those sprites from ruining the Magic Forest!

Azmina zoomed up beside her. "Where are we headed?" she asked. "Do you know what the Tree Queen meant by 'aim high'?"

"I figure she meant that we should go to the highest point in the forest," Naomi said.

She nodded to the mountain looming in the distance. "I'm thinking we go up there."

Willa flew up on Azmina's other side. "Isn't that a bit ... obvious?" she said. "I mean, aren't riddles more complicated than that?"

Naomi felt a little wriggle of doubt inside her, but she pushed it away. "It's only the first part of the riddle, remember. We also have to 'get to the root of the problems'."

"What does *that* mean, I wonder?" Azmina mused.

"We'll work that out when we get there," said Naomi. "Let's speed up. Who knows how long we've got until the sun sets!"

The mountain looked big from a distance. But as they flew towards the peak, Naomi realized it was enormous! The air grew icy cold and thin. Naomi felt that wriggle of doubt again as they came in to land. The top of the mountain was almost completely bare. The wind whipped across their glittering scales.

All Naomi could see were some rocks and a

huge leafless tree, its bare branches reaching for the sky. Naomi could feel the others watching her. She thought about the Tree Queen's riddle. *Find the one who seems calm but is actually petrified.* She knew that *petrified* was another word for "scared". But there was no one up here who was calm or scared. There was no one up here at all! What did the Tree Queen mean? Naomi wished she could ask her dad for help. When she got stuck on a riddle, he always came up with a hint to get her thinking right.

"Let's look around the tree," Naomi suggested. Maybe there was a little animal living there that they needed to find.

As Naomi circled the tree, one of her wings brushed against the trunk. She stopped. Had the tree just *shivered*? Naomi patted the tree again, and this time she was *sure* the tree moved. She placed a paw on its sturdy trunk. It wasn't like a normal tree. It felt harder and colder than wood.

There came a deep, hearty laugh. "Please don't do that!" said a voice. "People don't think that stone is ticklish, but it actually is."

The Glitter Dragons stared at one another, and then at the tree.

"Did you just speak?" Naomi asked the tree.

"Yes." The voice sounded hollow but relaxed.

"I've been expecting you. A little bird told me that my cousin, the Tree Queen, sent you."

"Wow, the Tree Queen is your cousin? Can you transform like she does?" Azmina asked.

"No, I stopped being able to do that long, long ago," replied the tree creakily. "Back before I hollowed out and turned to stone."

"You're made of stone?" Willa exclaimed.

"Yes. I am a petrified tree," said the tree proudly. "That's what it's called when wood turns to stone. I actually quite like it. I don't have problems with termites or woodpeckers any more. Turns out it's rather relaxing being made of stone."

Excitement shot through Naomi. She understood the queen's riddle! This tree was very calm, but it was also petrified!

"We are making a potion to stop the Shadow Sprites. Do you have anything we might use?" Naomi asked.

The tree creaked apologetically. "Nothing up here, I'm afraid. But if you went down to my roots, you might find something."

"Get to the root of the problem!" Azmina yelled happily. "That's perfect!"

"Is it OK if we dig around your roots to look?" Willa asked.

"Of course!" said the tree in its chill way. "Fly up to my top, and you'll see I'm hollow. Dive in. But do try not to tickle me as you go!"

Together, the Glitter Dragons flew up to the top of the tree and looked in. Sure enough, the trunk was completely hollow.

"You really think we're supposed to go in there?" asked Azmina.

Naomi had that tingly feeling she got when she knew the answer to a problem. "I'm positive. I'll go first."

Naomi tucked her wings in close and dove head first into the trunk. It was a bit like going down the covered slide at the adventure park, only faster. And she had no idea what lay at the bottom!

It wasn't dark, though. The inside of the tree

seemed to glow. The colours kept changing: first green, then a deep blue, then a rich red.

Naomi just managed to roll into a ball in time to do a somersault landing at the bottom. She stood up and looked around. She was in an enormous underground cavern! Now Naomi could see where the glowing colours were coming from. The cavern walls were encrusted with gemstones of every imaginable hue. Naomi had never seen anything so beautiful in her life!

Just then, Azmina landed on the ground with

a loud splat. Willa came shooting out moments later and landed right on top of Azmina. Laughing, the two Glitter Dragons quickly untangled their shimmering silver and gold wings before they stood up and looked around too.

"This place is amazing!" Willa cried.

"Great work, Naomi," said Azmina, patting her on the back with a wing. "I bet one of these gemstones is the first ingredient!"

Naomi had been thinking the same thing. "The question is, which one?"

She looked around the huge space. There was an area where the gemstones seemed to sparkle even more brightly. Naomi ran a paw lightly over

the surface of the shinier section. To her surprise,

the gems felt warm. And some were *really* warm.

Naomi moved her paw along the precious

stones. Warmer, warmer, warmer.

I bet I'm supposed to find the warmest one,

Naomi decided. She reached a gleaming blue

sapphire that was so hot, she could hardly touch it. As she moved her paw away, the sapphire tumbled from the wall. Without hesitation, Naomi caught it.

She held it carefully between her talons as she quickly opened her bag and pulled out the magic apple. The gem was very hot to hold!

Azmina and Willa hurried over. "Is that it?" Willa asked, her eyes wide with excitement.

"I'm sure it is," Naomi said.

She twisted the leaf at the top of the apple and opened it up. Steam rose from the sapphire as Naomi dropped it into the hollowed-out apple. When the gem hit the bottom, it exploded into glittering blue powder. Naomi clamped the apple's lid on so none of the magic powder escaped.

She turned to the others, grinning. "Our first ingredient. We did it!"

"So good!" said Azmina. "But...um...how do we get out of here?"

It was a very good question. The inside of the tree was too narrow for them to fly back up, and too smooth to climb. There didn't seem to be any other way out. They were trapped!

5

The Glitter Dragons flew around the cavern,
trying to find an exit. Surely there was a way
out. One side of the cavern was darker and
had fewer gemstones. Naomi flew over there.
Perhaps there was an exit hidden in the gloom?
She squinted up at the roof. Long, thick tree

roots dangled down. Were they growing out of a tunnel? She was pretty sure they were!

"Willa, Azmina!" Naomi called, her voice echoing around the vast space. "I might have found a way out."

Willa and Azmina flew over.

"Could we use those roots to climb back up?"

"Let's try it," Azmina said. "We've got to get out of here somehow."

Together, the friends flew up to the dangling tree roots. As they got closer, they saw the roots were all different colours – violet, emerald, orange and blue. Naomi reached up to grab hold of an orange one. But to her surprise, it grabbed hold of her!

This was no ordinary tree root. It wrapped around Naomi's paw tightly. Her heart thumping, Naomi tugged at the root with her other paw. No matter what she did, the root would not let go. Now that her eyes had got used to the gloom, she could see more clearly.

"Don't grab them!" she called urgently to her friends. "They aren't tree roots! They're snakes!"

"Too late!" Azmina wailed.

Naomi turned to see that both Azmina and Willa had been caught by the snakes. Even worse, the snakes were pulling the Dragon Girls up through the gap! Naomi could feel the fear building inside her. She did not like the idea of being taken anywhere by a snake!

Then the Tree Queen's second clue jumped into her mind. *Look for the ones who are feared but should be revered.* Naomi was pretty sure that *revere* meant "admire". Was it possible the queen had meant that they should admire these snakes? As the snake pulled her up through the gap, Naomi's mind whirred, thinking over the second part of the riddle: *they don't have a leg to stand on.* That was definitely true of snakes!

But *completely harmless*? Some snakes were very dangerous. Unless that wasn't what the Tree Queen had said. Maybe she'd said completely *armless*? Naomi couldn't help chuckling at that. She was now pretty sure that the second clue had just found them!

The snake gave one last tug on her front paw and then suddenly let go. Naomi went flying and landed with a bump on a smooth surface. She sat up and looked around. She was inside another cavern, but this one was smaller, and its walls were smooth and pearly white. *It's like being inside a giant egg*, thought Naomi.

She had the feeling she was being watched. And no wonder: in the room were several brightly coloured snakes! They slithered over one another and around one another, their scales gleaming as their flexible bodies made moving patterns.

"Good afternoon," said Naomi, thinking fast. "Thanks for the lift."

The snakes hissed in surprise. "No worriessss!"

Naomi paused. She wasn't really sure what to say to a bunch of snakes. "We have a lot in common. You guys are covered in lovely shiny scales, just like we Dragon Girls are. And snakes are cool! What other animal can smell with its tongue and listen with its bones?"

Naomi was *really* glad that she had paid attention on her recent school trip to the zoo. The snakes began to slither over to her.

"Oh, thisss glittery dragon issss ssssssooo charming!" they hissed in a delighted way. "Mosssst visitorssss are sssscared of ussss."

"Not me!" said Naomi firmly, although she actually *was* a tiny bit scared. Still, the snakes did seem quite friendly.

Just then, another snake appeared at the entrance, and Willa came tumbling into the space, quickly followed by Azmina. Naomi's friends gasped when they saw the snakes.

"It's fine!" Naomi reassured them. "I'm pretty sure the snakes are our second clue. And I think they will help us, if we ask nicely."

"Of coursssse we will help you, charming

rainbow dragon!" hissed the snakes. "What issss the problem? Do you need ussss to bite ssssomeone for you?"

Willa gave a little yelp of alarm.

"Oh no, nothing like that," Naomi said hastily. "We are trying to beat the Shadow Sprites."

The hissing suddenly became very loud. "Those Shadow Sprites keep trying to get into our lair to sssteal our gorgeoussss colourssss!" complained the snake closest to Naomi.

"Don't worry, we're making a potion to stop them," Naomi explained. "The Tree Queen sent us to you for the second ingredient."

"What do you need?" asked a neon-green snake.

"I'm not sure," Naomi admitted.

"It's probably something colourful," said Azmina, trying to smile at a purple snake that was doing a little dance, clearly attempting to impress her.

The snakes began to hiss loudly. It sounded like wind blowing through dry grass. "Venom," they whispered to one another. "Our venom issss rare, powerful and it matchessss the colour of our scalessss."

Naomi grinned. Multicoloured snake venom sounded *exactly* right. "How do we get it?" she asked. "And whose venom should we use?"

"Use mine!" said one snake. "It is a fetching shade of pink. And I am an excellent biter. Look at my lovely fangs!" The snake opened its mouth wide to reveal two very white, very sharp fangs.

"Ha!" scoffed another snake. "My fangs are much sharper. And I polish them every night.

See?" It also opened its mouth to show off its teeth.

Naomi could see that Willa and Azmina were not enjoying this contest very much. To be honest, neither was she! The sooner the venom catching was over, the better.

Quickly, she grabbed the magic apple from her bag and opened it up. She held it under the pink snake's fangs. A bright pink drop of venom fell into the apple, fizzing as it hit the sapphire powder at the bottom. Naomi  caught another drop from the green snake and then more drops from the other snakes around her. Soon the apple was half-full of swirling venom, the colours like a kaleidoscope.

Naomi screwed the lid back on and beamed at Azmina and Willa.

Two ingredients down, and only one to go!

6

Just then, Naomi heard a humming sound. When she turned, she saw a familiar bright blur of feathery colours. "Unichick!" she cried in delight. "How did you find us down here?"

"I will always find you, wherever you are!" chirped Unichick in her cheery sing-song voice.

"And right now, I have an urgent message. Time is running out, Glitter Dragons. The sun is setting fast, and the Shadow Sprites are getting longer and stronger by the moment. You must find the third ingredient as quickly as possible. If you don't, all the good work you three have done so far will be for nothing."

"Oh, don't go!" hissed the snakes.

"Thanks, but we really can't stay," Naomi said. "We must stop the Shadow Sprites before they destroy the Magic Forest."

The snakes hissed approvingly. "Yesssss! We sssssupport you." They started up a chant.

"Sssssnakes for dragonsss! Sssssnakes for dragonsss!"

Naomi shook her head and smiled. This was not an experience she'd forget in a hurry!

She tried to recall the final clue. *Sweetness is held within my skin. But I am protected by many a pin.*

Naomi felt her chest tighten. "I'm not sure about the final clue," she admitted to her friends. Sometimes, when Naomi's dad gave her a puzzle to solve, she found that thinking out loud helped.

"Sweetness held within a skin," she murmured. "What is sweet and has a skin?" Something jumped into her mind. "Fruit!" she cried.

Willa nodded excitedly. "Of course! That makes perfect sense!"

"But which fruit?" Azmina wondered. "I bet there are thousands of fruit trees in the Magic Forest."

Naomi turned her thoughts to the second part of the puzzle. What kind of fruit was protected by *many a pin*?

"BERRIES!" Naomi yelled the word so loudly that everyone jumped, including the snakes and poor little Unichick. "Blackberries and raspberries have prickles!" She turned to Unichick. "Is there a place where we can find berries growing?"

Unichick fluttered her feathers even faster. "The Berry Dale!" she trilled. "I know a short cut. Follow me!"

Unichick zoomed out of the snake den. Azmina and Willa followed. Naomi turned to the snakes and bowed. "Thank you for your

help," she said. "We couldn't have done this without you."

"Our pleasure, pretty glittery one!" hissed the snakes. "Back before the Shadow Queen started causing trouble, sssnakesss and dragonsss were friendsss in the Magic Foressst. We would like it to be that way again."

Naomi nodded. "You can count me as a friend! Goodbye and thanks again."

With that, Naomi raced off to catch up with the others.

❧

Unichick led the Dragon Girls through a winding series of tunnels. This wasn't easy. Sometimes the tunnels were so narrow the Dragon Girls had to wriggle along on their bellies.

"Right now I feel more like a Worm Girl than a Dragon Girl," Azmina joked.

Naomi laughed, then let out a quick glittery roar.

"Naomi? Everything OK?" Willa called.

"Just showing the Shadow Sprites we're not afraid of them!" Naomi called back.

The tunnel had grown very narrow – so

narrow that the dragons could barely squeeze through it at all.

"What's that?" Naomi yelped in surprise, looking up. Something had just dropped on the top of her head and dribbled down her face.

Naomi looked up. Liquid was dripping down from the earth above her. What *was* it?

Unichick's melodious voice rang out. "Don't worry – it's berry juice. We're just below the Berry Dale now. Here's the passageway that takes us up into the middle of the dale. Keep a lookout for Shadow Sprites, though!"

Naomi watched as first Unichick, then Willa and Azmina disappeared up through the passageway.

"Oh WOW!" she heard her friends exclaim. "This is AMAZING! Naomi, get up here quick!"

Of course, that made Naomi very curious! She took a deep breath and wriggled up through the narrow gap. Her friends and Unichick were hovering above her in the air. Naomi flew up beside them and looked down. She was expecting to see a field full of berries, and that was what she saw. But it didn't look anything like she'd imagined!

Naomi knew that berries were red or purple or blue. She had even seen white and yellow berries. But the berries in this field were every colour imaginable! There were turquoise berries, pale pink berries, dazzling gold berries. There were berries that glowed like moonlight, and berries that flashed on and off like lights. Some were the size of ping-pong balls. Naomi spotted a bright blue berry the size of a beach ball!

She couldn't resist flying down to touch a very pretty aqua berry.

As Naomi stretched out a paw, a swinging vine lashed at her. It was covered in gleaming needlelike prickles.

"Watch out!" warned Unichick.

Naomi just managed to move out of the way in time.

"Most berry plants in the Magic Forest are fierce," Unichick explained. "They won't give up their fruit easily. You must choose the right fruit carefully, for you will have only one chance."

Naomi gulped. Only one chance? No pressure or anything!

7

A tiny berry caught Naomi's eye. It looked like a droplet of water on a leaf, but Naomi could see that the berry was full of multicoloured juice. It was unlike any berry that existed in her normal world.

She felt Unichick fluttering next to her. "You've spotted the Rainberry," she said softly.

"That's a very rare fruit. It only grows every second season, and usually hides itself away. I think it wants you to pick it, Naomi."

Somehow Naomi thought so too. Carefully, she reached out a paw. The see-through skin of the berry looked fragile. She was scared she'd destroy this precious final ingredient! This time, no prickle-covered vines lashed out at her. In fact, the surrounding leaves seemed to part, to make it easier for Naomi to reach out.

Just as Naomi was about to take the berry, a grey shape flashed into view. A Shadow Sprite!

Before Naomi realized what was happening, the Shadow Sprite whipped the berry away and zoomed off!

"Catch that sprite!" cried Naomi, and the three Dragon Girls and Unichick rose into the air and dashed off.

The surrounding forest was dense and tangled. The Shadow Sprite was darting around trees and through bushes. The forest suddenly seemed very dark, making the sprite hard to follow. There was a rumble of thunder.

"Naomi, go on without us!" called Azmina. She sounded out of breath and very far away. "We're only slowing you down!"

"OK!" Naomi called back over her shoulder.

She didn't turn for fear of losing sight of the sprite. Her gymnastics training had sharpened her reflexes; she was definitely the most agile at flying. "I'll get that Rainberry back!" she called as lightning lit up the sky. She tried to sound cheerful, but inside, she was wishing she didn't have to do this alone.

"I'm here, don't forget," said a chirpy little voice beside her. "And I know you'll get that Rainberry!"

Rain had started to fall, but Naomi's heart swelled at Unichick's lovely words. It was true. She *wasn't* alone. But when the lightning flashed again, Naomi saw that Unichick's beautiful feathers had started to fade. Her normally bright tail was now grey! There was no time to lose.

The Shadow Sprite darted to the right, disappearing into a thick and gloomy patch of forest. Naomi and Unichick followed, weaving expertly between trees, over boulders, and around brambles.

It was impossible to see the Shadow

Sprite. But the Rainberry had begun to glow, changing from one hue to the next.

"It wants you to save it!" tweeted Unichick.

Naomi had the same feeling. She kept her eyes fixed on the changing colours of the berry, using them to guide her through the rain, which was now falling heavily.

The Shadow Sprite clutching the berry was fast and nimble. But so was Naomi. When the sprite tried to lose her by diving into a clump of stinging nettles, Naomi simply flew around the nettles and caught up on the other side. When it slipped between two low-hanging branches, Naomi used her tail to swing herself over the top of them. And when the sprite suddenly darted up into the treetops, Naomi used her powerful leg muscles to leap from branch to branch.

"You're getting closer!" chirruped Unichick excitedly.

It was true. The glowing Rainberry was almost within reach. Naomi felt the blood pumping through her body. She hardly noticed the rain pelting against her. The Shadow Sprite was now zigzagging as if it wasn't sure where to go next.

"Stop! Give me the Rainberry!" yelled Naomi.

She was close enough now that if she stretched out a paw, she might be able to hook the berry with a claw.

"Do it, Naomi!" cheered Unichick.

Naomi reached out and felt the creepy cold of the sprite. She flexed her claws, trying to grab at it, but the sprite slipped away and surged ahead. Staying focused, Naomi sped up again. Soon, she was once more upon the sprite. She reached forward. She almost had it...

Just then, lightning lit up the forest again. There were Shadow Sprites everywhere! They slid down from treetops and wriggled up tree trunks. Each time the lightning flashed, Naomi glimpsed more shadows dashing here and whooshing there.

Worst of all, they were heading right for her!

"Unichick, watch out!" Naomi cried as

the Shadow Sprites began to gather and swirl as one. Faster and closer they whirled, creating a tornado of shadows around Naomi and Unichick. Naomi had seen the Shadow Sprites do this underwater, but she'd never seen it in mid-air!

Naomi could just make out Unichick being buffeted from side to side. She grabbed the tiny bird, tucking her under one wing to keep her safe. She felt protective of her little friend, particularly now that she'd seen her grey tail. But holding her definitely made it harder to fly.

Naomi was getting tired. Worse, she could feel her spirits dropping. She had no chance of beating this many Shadow Sprites.

We try and we try, but the sprites just keep returning, Naomi thought.

She heard a nasty voice in her ear. "Just give up, Dragon Girl. We are too many. You'll never win."

"Don't listen, Naomi," sang little Unichick. "You can beat them."

Naomi tried to focus on what Unichick was saying, but the Shadow Sprites made her feel confused and hopeless. The swirling mass moved in tighter and tighter circles around her.

Their voices grew louder. "The others succeeded in their quests, but you will fail," they whispered.

It's true, thought Naomi. Sadness bloomed in her chest. She felt the cold rain seeping through her scales and into her heart. *I am going to let the others down. The Magic Forest will be overtaken, and it will all be my fault!*

"You know that what they're saying isn't true, Naomi!" chirped Unichick. She flew out from under Naomi's wing and hovered nearby.

"You must roar away your doubt. Roar away their mean words!"

Naomi drew in a breath. But the roar got caught in her chest. All that came out was a small puff of glitter that quickly washed away in the heavy rain.

"I can't," she sighed.

"Yes, you can!" insisted Unichick. "I know you can, and so does the whole forest. Listen!"

At first, all Naomi could hear was the whirling of the Shadow Sprites and their mean whispers. But then, very faintly, she heard ... birdsong!

It was soft but getting steadily louder. It kept changing too.

"It sounds like different birds are singing the same song," Naomi said. She'd never heard anything quite like it.

"The birds are passing along a message from your friends," explained Unichick. "They sang it to a bird near the Berry Dale, who sang it to another bird, and so on."

Naomi felt a tiny, welcome wave of warmth pass through her. Her friends had done that for her? In that case, she was *not* going to give up.

The birdsong drew closer, and even more birds joined in. The song grew so loud it began to drown out the mean whisperings of the Shadow Sprites.

Soon Unichick could make out the words, and she translated them from birdsong for Naomi:

Naomi's going to save the day

She will roar those sprites away!

The shadows might be sly and mean

But they're no match for the Dragon Girl team!

When Unichick began to sing it a second time, countless other birds joined in. Soon it felt like the entire Magic Forest was singing along! The warmth in Naomi flowed through her body, growing in strength. It was impossible to feel like a failure with her friends' gorgeous song ringing in her ears.

Naomi felt a roar building inside her. And it was built from happiness.

ROAR!

The shadow tornado blasted apart. Light filtered through, and shadows went flying in all directions. Naomi roared again, even louder this time.

ROARRRR!

The Shadow Sprites whirled off into the air. But Naomi knew she didn't have much time.

The Shadow Sprites were already regrouping. A big, menacing cloud of them was forming overhead.

The wind and the rain were loud, but Naomi thought she could hear the sound of beating wings. Was she imagining it? Then she heard a familiar voice. A moment later, a shower of golden glitter arced through the air.

Azmina landed beside her and flung a soggy wing around her. "We found you!"

Willa appeared in a flutter of water and silver sparkles. "We heard your roar. It was amazing!"

Naomi hugged her friends. "So was that birdsong!"

The song from her friends, and their arrival,

made Naomi feel strong – which was lucky because she still had to get that Rainberry! She spotted a tiny glowing dot, vanishing between the trees. Naomi dashed after it, but the Shadow Sprite holding it was way ahead.

Naomi prepared her biggest roar ever. The roar burst from her, glittering in all the colours of the rainbow. It covered the sprite, dissolving it to dust. The Rainberry began to fall towards the ground. Naomi leapt forward, the muscles of her shining, rainbow-striped body rippling.

You can do this, she told herself. She stretched out a paw ... and yes! The Rainberry dropped right into it! As Naomi's paw curled protectively around the precious fruit, the forest and the other Dragon Girls erupted into

birdsong and loud cheering.

Naomi flew back to her friends. She opened

her paw to reveal the Rainberry, which glowed

with all the colours of the rainbow.

"Wow, it's so beautiful," breathed Willa.

"Let's add it to the potion right away," said Azmina. "I don't like the look of that storm cloud one bit."

"Me neither!" agreed Unichick.

Naomi glanced up. That was no normal storm cloud. It was made of Shadow Sprites, but this time something seemed different. Naomi thought she could see a face in the shadows.

Quickly, Naomi pulled the magic apple from her bag and opened it. The mixture inside was now an awful sludgy colour. It reminded Naomi of when she mixed too many paints together in art class.

Naomi held her breath as she dropped the Rainberry into the potion. For a terrible moment, nothing happened. And then the potion began to bubble, like water in a pan. The grey sludge turned into a glorious swirl of colours! A sweet aroma filled the air. The Dragon Girls breathed in deeply.

"It smells like apple and mango!" Azmina sighed.

"Really? I smell pineapple and blueberry!" said Willa.

Naomi laughed. "All I know is, it smells amazing!"

Naomi felt proud, despite the strange and low-hanging cloud. They'd made the potion, and she knew it was perfect.

"What do we do with it now?" Azmina asked.

"I mean, how do we use it to stop the sprites and bring back all the colours of the forest?"

"I—I don't know," admitted Naomi. Her good feeling wilted.

"Maybe we should return and ask the Tree Queen?" suggested Willa.

Naomi shook her head. "We don't have time."

"Yes. It is too late, Dragon Girls," boomed a voice from above.

The Dragon Girls looked up. The voice seemed to come from the storm cloud itself.

"Am I imagining it," whispered Willa, "or is that cloud talking to us?"

"Sadly, you're not imagining it," muttered Naomi.

The thick, billowing cloud lowered until it was hovering above the ground. The vapour parted to reveal the figure of a woman. She was tall and thin, and her long, drapey dress seemed to be made of ribbons of smoke that rippled in the wind. Everything about her was grey. Naomi wasn't sure if she was very young or very old,  but she definitely looked mean. Atop her head rested a crown the colour of dust. It flickered in the wind, like tiny, ash-coloured candles.

Instantly, Naomi knew who this must be. "The Shadow Queen!" she cried.

9

A slow smile spread across the figure's face. She began to move forward. As she did, Shadow Sprites slid from the darkness and wrapped themselves around her like elegant scarves.

"Very good, Dragon Girl," the Shadow Queen said softly.

It felt like her words were being whispered right into Naomi's ear.

"The Tree Queen chose you three well. You have outsmarted my sprites. But you won't outsmart me." She stretched out a long, thin arm. "Give me that potion, Dragon Girl."

"Don't do it!" Willa called.

"No way," Naomi said. But she noticed that her arm didn't seem to be listening to her. In fact, her arm seemed to want to give the potion to the Shadow Queen!

"Never," Naomi said firmly. She was talking to her own arm more than to the Shadow Queen. She forced herself to put the lid back on the apple and tuck it into her bag.

It was like dragging herself out of bed early for gymnastics training. It took a lot of will power, but once the potion was safely away, Naomi felt stronger. "We know what you want to do. You want to make the forest grey and shadowy all the time."

The Shadow Queen's eyes glittered like

flint. "I suppose the Tree Queen told you how terrible we shadows are. But we're not so awful, you know. Everyone looks for us on a hot day when they want to escape the sun. You can tell what time of day it is simply by looking at us. And tell me, haven't you made shadow puppets against the wall with your hands?"

"Shadows are not *all* bad," agreed Naomi. "But we don't want the Magic Forest covered in them all the time. We like the sunshine and bright colours too."

"Well, I don't agree!" thundered the Shadow Queen. The whole forest seemed to quiver with fear. "Now, give me that potion."

She lunged at Naomi, who neatly

somersaulted out of the way. The Shadow Queen tried again and failed again. Now she looked *really* angry.

"Shadow Sprites! Come one, come all!" she called in a voice that was somehow very soft and very loud at the same time.

Suddenly the sky was full of shadows, zooming in from every direction. The arrival of their queen had made them stronger and faster.

The Dragon Girls launched into the air to face the swirling mass of Shadow Sprites. One Shadow Sprite broke away from the pack and dive-bombed Azmina, who swished it away with a powerful wing. Another one flew towards Naomi, who quickly somersaulted out of reach. Willa roared away a particularly cheeky sprite who was circling Unichick.

Naomi's stomach clenched tight with worry. The Dragon Girls were wet, tired and outnumbered. How long could they hold off the sprites?

The Shadow Queen swirled overhead, directing her Shadow Sprites like an army general.

Naomi tried to focus. There had to be a better way out of this than fighting. She watched as Willa shook her glorious, wet wings, flinging water into the air. The droplets of water shone as they caught the last glimmers of light in the sky.

Naomi stared at the droplets. Her heart began to beat very quickly. She had an idea. She pulled out the magic apple and took off the lid. The potion inside swirled like a kaleidoscope.

"Give that to me!" shrieked the Shadow Queen, lunging towards it.

"No way!" Naomi roared. Her rainbow glitter filled the air and settled into a bubble of colour protecting Naomi and her friends.

The Shadow Queen shrank back, but Naomi didn't think her glitter bubble would hold for long.

"Friends!" Naomi whispered. "This is our moment. I have an idea, but it's pretty wild."

"The wildest ideas are always the best," Azmina said firmly.

"Let's do this!" Willa agreed.

"My plan relies on each of our strengths. It will only work if we do this together. Willa, I need you to shake that silvery water from your wings, OK? And Azmina, I need you to roar your golden glitter."

"But why?" Willa asked.

"Because we are going to make a rainbow," Naomi explained softly. "Rainbows are made of water and light. Willa, you're giving us the water, and, Azmina, the glow of your golden glitter will create the light."

"And you'll roar in the colours!" Azmina finished, looking excited.

Naomi nodded. "And hopefully the potion will do the rest. Are we ready?"

Azmina and Willa nodded, their eyes gleaming.

Naomi turned to look at the Shadow Queen. Naomi steeled herself. They *had* to stop her. She took a deep breath and shouted, "One, two, three, GO!"

Willa shook her entire body, sending thousands of shimmering water droplets into the air. At the same time, Azmina and Naomi roared their loudest, most glittery roars. Azmina's golden glitter, Willa's silvery water droplets, and Naomi's rainbow glitter clashed like cymbals in mid-air and dropped into the potion.

The potion began to swirl around and around, like an invisible hand had stirred it. Naomi's hopes surged. Something was happening, she could feel it!

The Shadow Queen could clearly feel it too. "What are you doing?" she snarled, her hair and dress billowing furiously. "Stop that at once!"

But there was no stopping what the Dragon Girls had started.

A thin ribbon of colour curled out of the

potion and over their protective bubble. At first it glowed red, but as it snaked its way through the air, it began to stretch out. More colours appeared. Orange, then yellow, then green. Soon it glittered with all the colours of the rainbow.

"It's working!" Azmina yelled.

Willa flapped her wings excitedly. Naomi held her breath as the ribbon continued to rise through the air, growing ever wider and brighter. The darkness of the forest was banished. The birds immediately burst into song. Happiness surged through Naomi's chest. She beamed at her friends and saw that Willa and Azmina felt the same.

The surging colour arced up through the

air and towards the Shadow Queen and her sprites.

"Shadow Sprites! Attack the rainbow!" commanded the Shadow Queen, her voice booming like thunder.

The sprites darted at the multicoloured arch, but every time a sprite touched the rainbow, it dissolved into ash. The rainbow continued to grow longer, wider, and even more glorious. As Naomi watched, it lit up the cloud of Shadow Sprites, briefly illuminating the Shadow Queen in all the colours of the rainbow.

The Shadow Queen wailed in rage, and immediately began to fade. "You haven't seen the last of me," she growled in fury, before disappearing entirely.

High-pitched screeches filled the air as the last of the Shadow Sprites crumbled and disappeared.

10

The Dragon Girls and little Unichick turned to one another, huge smiles on their faces.

"That was amazing!" Azmina cried, clutching at her chest.

Naomi reached out to touch the rainbow that she and her friends had made. She thought her paw would pass right through it, but the rainbow felt surprisingly solid. It was smooth, like the surface of a slide, but as warm as a shaft of sunlight.

Naomi turned to her friends, a new idea forming. "Let's follow our rainbow! I have a hunch about where it will lead."

"We can try, but my wings are still wet," said Willa. "I am not sure how well I can fly."

Naomi leaned against the rainbow, thinking. But the moment she touched the rainbow, she began to slide up its surface. "It's like a rainbow escalator!" she whooped.

"That's beyond cool!" Azmina laughed.

"Even more fun than the big waterslide at the pool!" Willa added.

Azmina and Willa leapt at the rainbow after Naomi. Suddenly, all three Glitter Dragons were whooshing along its colourful length.

"I wish we could do this in the normal world!" Willa cried.

"Me too!" Azmina yelled.

"Look!" Naomi cried.

Naomi thought her heart might explode with joy. Brightly coloured pearls of water were pouring down from the rainbow. The parts of the Magic Forest that had been ash grey were returning to their original colours. In fact, they looked even brighter now! The trees, the grasses, the flowers – everything looked freshly painted.

"It's working!" Naomi murmured to herself. She wanted to remember this feeling for ever.

When the Glitter Dragons reached the top of the rainbow's arch, they paused and looked around. The birds were singing joyfully, and Naomi could hear the happy sounds of other animals in the forest below.

Naomi gazed across the land stretching out before them. There was no sign of the Shadow Queen, and the sprites had all disappeared. They had done it! They had defeated them.

"Look, there's the glade!" Azmina pointed towards the end of the rainbow.

Sure enough, there was the glowing heart of the forest, with its shimmering protective force field.

"OK, team. Let's go!" Naomi cried.

Sliding up the rainbow had been fun, but sliding down it almost took Naomi's breath away. It was so fast! The warm wind whooshed past her and she felt the happiness build until a glittery roar burst out of her. When Azmina and Willa heard it, they joined in. The air swirled with gold, silver, and rainbow glitter.

The rainbow ended where the glade's force field began. The Dragon Girls slid easily through the force field and tumbled on to the glade's soft grass.

Naomi sprang to her feet. The glade was protected from evil, so it had always been beautiful. But the grass seemed even more lush, the flowers more vibrant.

And best of all was the Tree Queen! She was covered in blossoms and bright green leaves. Naomi had never seen her look like this. Her smile dazzled them. "Welcome back, Glitter

Dragons! This quest was the hardest yet. My birds tell me that you came face-to-face with the Shadow Queen herself! But you succeeded. You have returned balance  to the forest. I couldn't be more proud."

Naomi, Azmina, and Willa grinned at one another. Nothing felt better than being praised by the Tree Queen!

"We're a pretty good team, aren't we?" said Naomi, reaching out her paw.

"The BEST!" agreed Azmina and Willa, bumping their paws against hers.

Was that the world's first dragon paw bump?
Naomi wondered.

A brightly coloured bird landed on one of the Tree Queen's flowering branches. It sang a short, cheerful song, and the queen nodded. "Your potion worked perfectly, Dragon Girls. The Shadow Sprites have gone, and the Shadow Queen is sorely weakened."

Naomi's heart sank a little at this news. "The Shadow Queen is still around?"

"We saw the rainbow destroy her!" cried Azmina.

The queen smiled gently. "I know you did. But it's not that easy to get rid of a shadow.

And anyway, we will always need them. Our task is to keep everything in balance."

"Does the Shadow Queen know that?" Willa asked.

"She knows it, but she doesn't like it," replied the Tree Queen. "Which is why the Magic Forest will always need Dragon Girls. Now it's time for you to return to your homes. But first, here is a gift from the Magic Forest. It's our way of saying thank you."

The Tree Queen shook a branch and three things came tumbling down. For Azmina, there was a bracelet with a little golden leaf pendant. Another bracelet fell in front of

Willa. It had a tiny silver shell dangling from it. Naomi's had a flower, each petal a different colour. The charm bracelets were beautiful, and perfect for each of them. The Dragon Girls each put theirs on. Naomi handed back the special bag she had been wearing.

She felt a bit sad about leaving.

The Tree Queen seemed to read her mind. "I am always here, in my glade," she said. "You can visit me any time, if you want?"

The Dragon Girls exchanged excited glances. Of course they would like to visit again!

"See you at school?" said Azmina, getting ready to leave the glade.

Naomi nodded, her sadness all gone. Their quest had ended, but their friendship definitely hadn't! This thought kept her warm as she stepped out of the glade's force field and spotted her special flower. She paused to smell it before tucking it behind her ear.

She took a deep breath and leapt into the air, flapping her powerful wings to give herself plenty of height. She somersaulted wildly, feeling a magical whoosh of air. Her skin tingled as she morphed back into girl form. Then, curling into a ball, she spun through the air...

A moment later, Naomi landed firmly on two

feet that were very much human. The sound of kids playing nearby was loud and familiar and wonderful.

"Naomi! You must be starving!" Naomi's mum called. "Come and eat something before the food's all gone."

Naomi was back in the adventure playground, near the stone wall. Her mum had Naomi's cute baby brother on one hip. Dakari gave a gleeful clap at the sight of his beloved sister.

Naomi skipped over. "I am starving," she said. "I'll just be one sec."

She waited until her mum had turned away and then reached for the flower charm on her bracelet. She gave it a quick kiss.

"Thanks for everything, Magic Forest," she whispered. "I sure hope to see you again soon."

Turn the page for a special sneak

peek of Azmina's adventure!

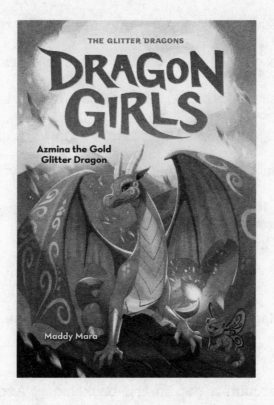

Azmina lay on her stomach in her brand new garden. The weather was warm for autumn, but Azmina didn't feel the sun on her skin. She didn't notice a dog barking nearby. She didn't even hear her mum singing as she unpacked boxes in the house they had just moved into.

A strange sound had caught Azmina's attention. The sound blocked out everything else. It was as if someone was whispering the first line of a song.

Magic Forest, Magic Forest, come explore...

Through a gap in the back fence, Azmina

could see the edge of a forest. Was the music coming from there?

Azmina wasn't used to lying around on the grass, admiring trees. She thought of herself as a city girl, through and through. Well, she used to, anyway. She wasn't quite sure who she was in this new place yet. Back in the city she was always on the go: singing lessons, playing football with her friends, organizing sleepovers.

But now, there wasn't anyone to organize sleepovers with. Everything had changed when she and her mum moved. Azmina liked the kids at her new school, but she didn't have any besties yet.

In school, she had been assigned to a table

with two other girls named Willa and Naomi. Somehow Azmina just knew that she was meant to be friends with them. She could feel it, fizzing like bubbles in a soft drink, deep in her stomach. But she wasn't quite sure how to make it happen.

Azmina sighed. She knew that friendships took time, but she hated being the new girl.

Magic Forest, Magic Forest, come explore...

Azmina sat up. The singing was clearer now. It was definitely coming from the forest! But it was different from any music

Azmina had heard before. The melody was
like the songs of a
thousand birds and
the babble of a
river all mixed
together with the
rustling of leaves.

Azmina jumped up
and ran to the back fence. She
leaned over to get a closer look. Because she
was from the city, she'd never seen a real
forest up close before. She couldn't take her
eyes off it! The leaves had turned the colours
of autumn. These were Azmina's favourites –
brilliant red, fiery orange, and best of all,

bright yellow. The forest floor looked like it was covered with treasure.

There was one tree that caught Azmina's attention. It was the tallest of all, with long and graceful branches. The tree's leaves shone as if they were made of pure gold. Azmina felt a little shiver of excitement run up her back. There was something special about that tree. Something magical.

As she gazed into the forest, Azmina realized there were other curious things about it.

"I can smell flowers," Azmina muttered to herself. "But that doesn't make sense! Most of the flowers are gone now that it's autumn."

But that wasn't even the strangest thing. Azmina thought she could smell pineapples and mangoes. Azmina didn't know much about forests, but she was pretty sure pineapples and mangoes didn't grow around here!

Now that she was closer, Azmina could hear more singing coming from the forest.

Magic Forest, Magic Forest, come explore.

Magic Forest, Magic Forest, hear my roar!

Hear my roar? What could that mean?

Azmina repeated the words out loud, softly at first: "Magic Forest, Magic Forest." But each time

she said them, her voice got louder. One of the

golden leaves on the tallest tree spun up into

the air. It danced through the sky, swishing this way and that, leaving a glowing trail behind it.

Azmina watched as the leaf looped its way closer. When the leaf was above her, she leapt up and grabbed it. It was warm from the sunlight. Azmina's fingertips tingled.

Suddenly, she knew just what to do. Her voice rang out strong and true as she began to sing:

Magic Forest, Magic Forest, come explore.
Magic Forest, Magic Forest, hear my roar!

Instantly, a hot gust of wind swirled around her. Azmina closed her eyes as she was whooshed up into the air, spun around, and then dropped down on to the ground again. It took only a few seconds, but Azmina knew something amazing had happened. Something life-changing.

❧

Azmina opened her eyes to see that she was no longer in her garden. Instead, she was standing in the middle of the forest. Up close, it was even more beautiful than it had seemed from her garden. Vines twisted around tree trunks, heavy with fruits Azmina had never seen before. Flowers of every possible colour covered the ground like a carpet. Birdsong filled the air around her.

Azmina noticed a tiny, fuzzy pink ball attached

to a nearby vine. As she watched, the ball began to grow – right before her eyes! Within seconds, a perfect, ripe fruit had formed. It looked like a peach but smelled like raspberries. Azmina couldn't resist picking it and taking a bite. To her surprise, it tasted exactly like chocolate!

What was this place?

The tropical smells tickled her nose, and soon Azmina felt a sneeze building up. Azmina opened her mouth, threw back her head, and … *ACHOO!* She just loved sneezing! It always felt like scratching a troublesome itch.

Golden sparks fluttered down around Azmina. She looked at the glittering mist in surprise. Had she done that with her sneeze?

Azmina's heart pounded wildly. Something amazing was going on. But what, exactly?

Through the trees, Azmina spotted a shimmering lake. Azmina decided to check it out, and started to jog towards it. She had always been a fast runner, but today her legs felt stronger and faster than ever before. Soon, she was sprinting through the trees at top speed. She reached the lake in no time.

Skidding to a stop at the lake's edge, Azmina peered in. What she saw in the water made her gasp. Staring back at her from the watery surface was some kind of magnificent creature.

Azmina leapt away from the lake. She whipped around to face whatever it was that

was standing behind her. But she was all alone. She looked from left to right. Nothing. Maybe the creature was under the water? Or maybe she'd imagined the whole thing? Azmina crept back to the lake and looked in once more.

THE GLITTER DRAGONS

DRAGON GIRLS

We are Dragon Girls, hear us ROAR!

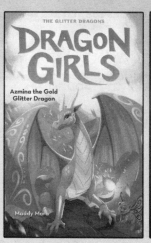

Read all three clawsome Glitter Dragon adventures!

ABOUT THE AUTHORS

Maddy Mara is the pen name of Australian creative duo Hilary Rogers and Meredith Badger. Hilary and Meredith have been collaborating on books for children for nearly two decades.

Hilary is an author and former publishing director, who has created several series that have sold into the millions. Meredith is the author of countless books for kids and young adults, and also teaches English as a foreign language to children.

The Dragon Girls is their first time co-writing under the name Maddy Mara, the melding of their respective daughters' names.